Cheryl Bealer Wynton

Murder Burger

Redrum Books

Cover by Goran Delic

ISBN 0615719864

First Edition 2012

ONE

I was never little.

At least that's what my mom tells people.

I remember the first time I heard her say it.

I was five years old going down the slide by myself.

"Is that your little girl?" someone at the park asked.

"Please, Cheyenne has never been little," I heard her say.

At the time I had felt proud. I was a big girl. No more sippy cup. No more stroller.

It wasn't until years later that I realized Mommy thought I had thunder thighs.

So that's why every morning she serves me a half slice of

grapefruit and a Fat Burner Energy Pill.

I'm not a pig, really.

I do the vegetarian thing, just like Mom does. I always drink diet soda and ask for the low-calorie salad dressing. (Except it pisses me off how they look at me sometimes, like yeah, you'd better get the low-cal, honey.)

It's just that I have my weaknesses.

Like the Cheez-its I keep under my bed for those urges at 2 a.m. or right after school or right after work.

Oh yeah, work. That's how this whole thing got started.

You see, I work for my dad at his restaurant.

I should say slave because for what he pays me he'd only get an illegal immigrant for like 15 minutes.

"Dad, it's Friday, everyone else got a check, where's mine?" I ask.

"I don't buy everyone else braces and freaking prom dresses!"

My dad is crazy. He actually thinks someone will ask me to

the prom.

Anyway, Dad owns this rundown hole of a burger joint off Interstate 9 called Monster Burger and it's where you'll find me Thursday through Sunday. Since the divorce, when I was 9, those have been my Dad Days.

Monday through Wednesdays, those are my Mom Days. So take your pick—packing burgers or popping diet pills—either way it all kind of sucks.

That Thursday was a typical Dad Day. He picked me up after school in his rusty old truck right in the bus zone so old Mrs. Butler had to come out and scream at him to move and half the school could see that a) not only am I not cool enough to drive myself to school b) my dad has a crappy car he can't even park half a block away like all the other sane parents.

Worse yet, he had to plant a big wet kiss on my cheek while people were still smirking at us. But that's Merle Margarini: big, loud, affectionate Italian. I don't mind the curly dark hair and the nice olive complexion he gave me, but the big I could do without.

"How was school?" he pulled away from the so obviously red curb.

"It sucked."

I didn't bother to tell him that Nicholas Sheridan talked Eric Shaw into trading seats with him in science so he could sit by me. Bye-bye beautiful Eric with the blue-black hair and huge dark eyes that don't even need eyeliner. I love the way his eyes crinkle when he smiles. I love the way that lock of hair always falls into his eyes. But I don't get to look at Eric anymore.

No, I'm stuck with Nicholas: zit-face, buckteeth and glasses. The same moronic face I've been looking at since I was 10 years old. It wasn't so bad back when we used to play tag and –I'll admit it—a little you show me yours I'll show you mine in the backyard. But it's been 7 years and the same old jokes are getting old.

Okay, the thing you need to know about Monster Burger is that up until two months ago it was called QuikBurger and this monster thing is a total joke. Dad hired some old guy named Hank to paint this "scary" monster on a piece of wood. It looks like Oscar the Grouch with a bad case of gingivitis.

He tacked this monster thing up over the QuikBurger sign then he had old Hank wall off part of the dining room and make it into a kiddie area complete with a ball pit. In case you don't remember, a ball pit is a big tub filled with plastic balls. A place where babies lose their diapers and junkies lose their needles.

After that, he had all the cups, napkins and menus outfitted with the little Monster guy that I like to call Gummy. But the worst thing is the shirt. It was bad enough when I had to wear stripes and a bow tie but now I walk around with a big green monster on my chest. Shoot me now.

When we got to the restaurant Eric was already in the backroom stocking condiments. Yeah, in addition to having biology with the guy I have to work with him. Extra time to stare at the back of a neck I'll never get to drape my arms around. Can't say that I can complain, though. He even looks cute in his Monster Burger T-shirt.

Sheila was out front stocking cups. She's new to our school this year and she's super cool—not phony like most stuck up girls. She talks to you like a real person whether you're popular or not.

Sheila says her dad's from Peru and her mom's Puerto Rican. She has beautiful wavy hair and skin the color of café latte. She's big—but in all the right places. A couple of skinny cheerleaders tried to dis her at first but the guys got on their case real fast. Sheila is too nice and funny not to like.

"What's up, Chey!" Sheila greeted me with a smile. She's the only one who calls me that, but I wish more people would cause it sounds cool.

"Hey, Shei," I answered.

"Billy Joe's in the back, didja see?"

Billy Joe was our code-name for Eric because we both think he looks like Billy Joe Armstrong from Green Day.

"Yeah, I saw."

"You should try talking to him sometime," she raised her thick eyelashes at me.

"No," I chuckled. "I'm not like you…"

"Girl, you're exactly like me, what are you…150?"

I stared at her.

"Pounds," she clarified impatiently.

"160," I lied.

"Okay, so we're almost exactly the same weight, all that's different is our attitudes."

I wanted to bust up laughing—like attitude is going to make Eric like me--but instead I said, "I never thought of it that way."

She's about to get on her attitude soapbox but I could tell from Merle's stink-eye that he wanted me to get behind the counter and get to work.

As I made my way back through the employee gate, I saw Eric peering at the buttons on the cash register.

I surprised him as I walked up.

"Trying to get some cash?" I joked, not meaning to sound

like such a bitch.

"Hey, I was just wondering how this thing works."

He seemed nervous and I noticed even more how blue his eyes were under the black mop of his hair.

"It's not that hard, actually," I explained with my heart beating out of my chest. "You just have to press this button after each item and then at the end press sale."

"Cool," he smiled and I saw that his front tooth is a tiny bit chipped and my heart skipped a little more.

"We should trade places sometime. I'll show you how to sling burgers and I'll try to work this thing," he suggested.

"I already know how to make burgers," I said quickly then bit my lip. Dummy. He wanted to show me something and I just kicked him to the curb. Visions of him guiding my hand onto the spatula went down the drain like so much grease.

"Oh yeah, right," he said with a smile. "I mean you were practically born here."

For the next half-hour I stressed about the Eric thing and without noticing

it I started a very intricate portrait of him and his guitar on my order pad.

It gets like that at Monster Burger. Slow. For long periods of time. I don't mind it that much because my sketches are getting better, and I can always get my homework done.

A beefy hand plunked down on my drawing and I looked up, startled.

"Whatchya drawing Moo Cow?"

It's Dirk. Quarterback, asshole. Sure, he's blonde but I don't know what the girls see in him. With his potbelly and jowls he would look 35 if it weren't for his letterman jacket.

I pulled on my order pad but he ripped it out of my hands. He looked at it and giggled, then grabbed my pen and scribbled something on my drawing.

I was just about to let him have it when he held his artwork up. He had turned Eric's guitar into a very lame looking cow.

"You jerk!" I said, trying to snatch back the drawing but he yelled toward the back, "Hey, Shaw, Moo Cow wants to do you!"

Don't cry, I told myself. I haven't cried since Destiny Fines and Melissa Klempner came up to me on the playground in fifth grade and asked me in those tittering voices, "Why are you so fat?"

This time I didn't cry, I just leaned over the counter, grabbed for that drawing and tried to scream Dirk's name but all that came out was a hoarse growl.

"Huh," he chuckled. "You even sound like a cow."

I heard a ripping sound and suddenly my Dad was standing there with half my drawing and Dirk's cup in his hands.

"Get lost, punk," he said through clenched teeth.

"Hey, that's my soda, man," Dirk whined.

Dad emptied the soda into the fountain drain, wadded the cup up in his hand and threw it into the garbage, all while giving Dirk his best Clint Eastwood glare.

Dirk looked like he might cry as he turned to Josh and said, "Come on, the food here sucks, anyway!"

As Dirk and Josh stomped out like petulant three-year-olds, Dad handed me my torn drawing.

"I know a guy who could off that son-of-a-bitch for you, only cost a month's salary, whaddya say?" he said, only half-joking.

"What salary?" I retorted.

I crumpled up the drawing and shot it into the garbage can, right onto Dirk's cup.

"My God, it's six o'clock! Where is everybody?!" Dad broke the silence of the last hour as he looked about the virtually empty dining room.

As if on cue, the bell on the front door tinkled as a little old lady and her even older husband shuffled in.

Even though my dad is pretty old himself, he seems to hate the elderly. He calls them "gray hairs" and complains about how little they buy and how long they take to eat.

But if it weren't for old people, half our business would be gone. Even though I'm sure our food hastens their deaths, old people are our most loyal customers.

"Good evening," I could tell he was trying hard not to sound irritated.

"I liked this place better when it was called QuikBurger," the old lady said to no one in particular. "Who wants to eat a Monster Burger, anyway? What's wrong with cow meat?"

"I'm sure you'll find our burgers are made with nothing but the finest Grade A beef!" he sounded like a commercial. "Now what can I get for you this evening, ma'am?"

"Coffee, black," the old lady barked back.

"Coffee, coming right up!" he turned to get the cup, but I could hear him under his breath, "I spend $5,000 remodeling this place and all she wants is coffee…"

"On second thought," the lady interrupted his mutterings. "Make that a cup of hot water to go."

I halfway expected him to throw the cup at her but he just smiled, handed her the cup and said a little too sweetly, "There's hot water in that urn over there…"

The old lady tottered off toward the drink station.

"Oh, don't you just want to see them choke sometimes?" he whispered through clenched teeth to no one in particular.

It was a typical night. A few more old people. One cop. Some truckers. Deader than a cemetery on a Saturday night.

I can deal with the boredom; it's just knowing that *he's* in the backroom that drives me crazy. If I'm lucky and somebody orders a burger I get to look at him for a split second through the service window. Sometimes it seems like his eyes linger just a second more than they have to. But I don't know if he's waiting for me to make a move or if he's just trying to remember if he put pickle on top of the lettuce.

And then there's Nicholas. He flits around me all night telling dumb jokes like the one about the guy who dug up Beethoven's grave only Beethoven was decomposing, get it? Not. The rest of the time he's in the bathroom rubbing spray-on tan all over his face. I think he's just trying to cover up his acne, but doesn't he realize having the complexion of a kumquat isn't much of an improvement?

When the last Formica tile is mopped and the last tub of tomatoes is put away, we could finally clock out.

There was a dark van waiting to pick up Sheila. Nicholas hopped on his bike and Eric slowly sauntered toward the highway.

"Dad," I whispered. "Can't we—"

I nodded toward Eric who was almost out of the parking lot.

"What? Him? Let him walk. Maybe it'll build him a little character under that frou-frou haircut."

I rolled my eyes but I didn't push it. The last thing I wanted to do was sit between Eric and my dad and listen to another rant about character.

On the drive home, I stared out the window at the dark nothingness. After my folks divorced, Dad insisted on buying a house in the boondocks. He said he wanted to be closer to the restaurant. I think he just wanted to be farther away from my mom.

As he drove, he whipped out his cellphone and dialed. It scares me when he does this because he's not such a good driver even without a phone glued to his ear.

"If you can just spot me a grand that'll put me through til next month, Charlie, whaddya say?"

Uncle Charlie is a veterinarian but when he got divorced he lost the lease on his office and now he drives around in a van neutering dogs and cats in supermarket parking lots.

"Whattya mean you're broke?!" he replied angrily. "Mom and Dad flushed 12 years of tuition down the toilet sending you to college!"

That's another thing. He gets mad if I get one B on my report card and yet he always complains that doctors and lawyers are no smarter than regular people. I told him that since regular people get B's maybe I could still be a doctor or lawyer. He didn't think that was too funny.

"No, I didn't go to the cemetery, Charlie...jeez, you still

believe all that superstitious mumbo jumbo?"

Just then I saw a large, dark shape in the road and we were headed straight for it.

As the headlights bore down, I could make out two glowing red eyes.

"Dad, watch out!" I yelled.

He slammed on his brakes, burning rubber as we skidded sideways. There was a loud thud as we crashed into whatever was in the middle of the road.

The car came to a stop.

"Are you okay?" he yelled, hands still clenched to the steering wheel.

"Yeah, but we hit something."

"I know." As he answered I noticed blood on his lip. "You stay here, I'm going outside."

Before I could tell him to wait, he was out the door. My door was stuck. On the other side of my window, heavy panting and snorting. I looked out and saw two horns and hooves, some kind of farm animal. It looked up at me and I gasped. Two glowing red eyes filled up the window. I wanted to scream but my throat felt paralyzed.

Dad came around the corner of the truck and the beast's low, guttural growling filled the air. I willed myself to speak, pound on the window--anything, but instead I watched in frozen fear as the thing lunged at him. He shrank back, yelling in pain and holding his arm.

"Daddy!" I finally found my voice.

The creature turned slowly and looked back at me. Eyes still aglow, it pawed the ground, about to charge.

"The gun!" he yelled. "Get the gun out of the glove box!"

"What?" I said, rolling down the window, hearing him, but not understanding.

"Cheyenne, get the fucking gun!"

I opened the glove box and saw something there, black and dangerous. I didn't dare touch it. I'd never seen a gun that close before, never even knew my dad kept one in there.

"Cheyenne, now!" he yelled, and then turned to run as the thing in front of him pawed the ground, getting ready to charge.

I grabbed the pistol, aimed for the cow and pulled the trigger. A deafening crack, then the animal stopped in its tracks. I pulled the trigger again and this time the beast's legs crumbled beneath it. I was about to let loose some more rounds when my dad crawled up beside me into the cab and grabbed the gun.

"Here, let me finish this bastard off," he said, and with both hands fired right at the demon-cow's head. It fell over.

I sank into my dad's arms, crying.

"You done good," he said patting my back. "Thank God for semi-automatic weapons."

TWO

I don't know how long we stayed there in the cold cab of my dad's truck, me freezing in my Monster Burger T-shirt and him pacing around outside with the cellphone to his ear.

"Shouldn't we call the cops?" I called to him through the window.

He completely ignored me.

"Yeah, Charlie," he was talking to my uncle again. "I hit the jackpot, literally. A cow, Charlie…I just blew its brains out…what? It tried to kill me….listen, it's a long story, I'll tell you everything. But first I want to know if you still have those butchering tools? Good. Just get over here as soon as you can…I'm on Highway 11 off the Buttonwillow Exit…"

I couldn't believe it. He was going to make me wait in the cold car just so he and Uncle Charlie could come cut up some stupid cow.

"Can you drive me home?"

"What, huh, yeah, sure, honey" he said absent-mindedly as he was putting his phone away. "Just as soon as Uncle Charlie gets here."

I didn't end up getting home until about four in the morning.

I hid in the cab of the truck and pretended to sleep while Uncle Charlie buzzed away with his saw.

How could they actually think of butchering that thing for meat?

What if it came back to life like some kind of zombie? I thought. After all, it was no ordinary cow. Not with those red eyes and nasty disposition.

By the time I convinced myself that zombies only exist in movies, my dad was shaking my shoulder, waking me up for school.

He looked like hell. Pale, with a day's growth of beard. And neither of us wanted to talk about what had happened the night before.

I got to school late and slept through the rest of the day.

Lunch was even a blur until Sheila came up to me.

"Could you do me a big favor, chica?" she said, grabbing my arm in that way that made me feel like I was almost her best friend.

"It depends on what it is."

"Tell your dad I can't work tonight, there's a game and Miss Brown said if I miss one more I'll get cut from baton squad."

"Why don't you tell him yourself?" I said, not so nicely. I wanted to be her friend but I was tired of always having to make excuses for her.

"I can't," she moaned. "I called in sick like three times this month and I think your dad's gonna can my ass."

"Oh, he wouldn't do that," I lied.

"Wait!" she squeezed my arm even tighter. "Don't tell him I

have a game…tell him something to make him feel really sorry for me."

"Like what?"

"I don't know--like someone died or something. You'll think if something…you're really smart."

After school, instead of the rusty old truck in the red zone, I saw my mom's sleek, shiny Acura. Different taste in cars. Same shitty parking skills.

"Where's Dad?" I asked as soon as I got in the car.

"He called and said he was too sick to come today," she said. "Aren't those the same clothes you had on yesterday?"

Like she's one to talk. My mom wears the same thing everyday: shiny leggings, a T-shirt that says "Ask me about Fat-Burner Energy!" and a pastel headband around her forehead. Where dad and I are dark, she is bleach blonde, her fair skin tinged to a tanning-bed bronze. Dad said Mom used to be plump like me, but now her legs are twigs and her arms are like two muscular branches, no fat allowed to rest on her calorie-burning body.

"We had a late night last night."

I stopped short of sharing all that business about the cow. She'd just freak out and drag my dad back into court for more visitation rights. As if sitting around her condo listening to her bitch about my thighs counts as visitation.

"So that's why he called in sick," she muttered. "Probably had you up all night drinking milkshakes and playing poker...well, that's why we have to make an extra-long stop at the Butterfly Club."

The Butterfly Club is the old ladies' gym where my mom works. She teaches them lame dance moves to Ricky Martin songs and they kid themselves that they're exercising.

"God, Mom, I'm supposed to work tonight--can we just skip it?"

"You are not working one more night at that place; I thought we agreed 15 hours a week was enough.

"But I have to work for Sheila."

She took her hands off the wheel to throw them up in the air.

"Not the baton twirler!" she cried. "You should be the one out there twirling your stick, not her!"

I wanted to hit my mom so bad right then.

"Besides, it would be good exercise for you!"

I wanted to hit her even more after that remark, but I figured she'd probably run the car off the road and we'd both be killed.

Instead I kept my mouth closed. Except for the Fat Burner Energy Pill she made me wash down with a big slug of wheatgrass juice.

And then I went to the Butterfly Club, squeezed myself into ridiculous tights that made me look like a giant blueberry and did idiotic movements to bad disco music.

It was Kick-Dancing Night. I know what you're thinking, don't I mean Kick-Boxing? No. Nothing that cool. Kick-dancing is where you do a couple of knee-high kicks and pseudo-karate punches then you sashay across the floor and do some kind of bump and grind thing like a pole dancer. It wouldn't be so bad if I didn't have to watch old ladies do it. Not only is it gross to watch wrinkled flesh jiggle unnaturally in spandex, but what if somebody broke a hip?

Yet as I watched my mom chirping out her commands I started to get really into the kicking and punching part.

"Whoa, Cheyenne, look at you go!" she squealed.

You go Mom, I thought, as I pounded the air with my fist.

After our showers and--you guessed it--more pills and wheatgrass juice, I asked her if she could finally drop me off at Monster Burger.

"What? So you can wolf down a 1,000 calorie meal? No way, sweetie," she said over the din of the blow dryer.

"Mom, we at least have to call Dad, he's going to be short a counter clerk and I don't want Sheila to get blamed."

"Honestly, I don't know what you see in that girl," she sniffed. "My hairdresser says her family isn't even in this country legally."

I ripped the blow dryer cord out of the wall. She stared at me like I had unplugged her best friend.

"Sheila is my friend. She doesn't care how much I weigh or how many calories I eat," I hissed in a coarse whisper. "She treats me better than you do so if I want to fill in for her, I'll bloody well fill in for her."

We didn't say anything to each other on the way over to Monster Burger.

I was too mad and I think Mom was too afraid.

But just before I opened the door to get out, she ignited another bomb.

"Call me when you get off."

"I want to go home with Daddy tonight," I said icily.

"Cheyenne, technically, I know it's a Daddy Night, but, you're coming home with me," she said, matching the frost in my voice cube for cube.

"How about if there's no more Mommy Night and no more Daddy Nights, OK, I'm not eleven years old anymore! How about just Cheyenne nights? I decide where I want to sleep and right now that is as far away from you as I can possibly get."

I could tell she was about to say one more thing but I got out and slammed the door in her face before she could say another word.

She must have been really mad because instead of rolling down the power window and yelling at me she just put the car in drive and squealed off.

I didn't care.

I pulled my cap down low and marched across the parking lot hoping no one would talk to me.

I passed by a van. A girl and a guy were propped against it making out. I looked away in disgust as I realized the guy was Dirk. God, who would let that Neanderthal put his dog-lips on their mouth anyway?

I felt a hand on my shoulder and whirled around. It was Sheila, out of breath, lipstick smeared.

"Sheila?" I said, shocked. "Were you--"

"Hey, can you bring me out a plate of fries?" she ignored my glares behind her shoulder as Dirk gave me a caustic wave.

"I thought you had a baton competition," I asked accusingly.
"I did. I got first place! Listen, we gotta be at the game in like half an hour and I'm STARVING."

"Well, I have to get inside and work your shift, Sheila."

"Yeah, thanks so much…and try not to put so much salt on the fries."

Of course the dining room was empty.

That was nothing new.

But it was strange not seeing my dad behind the counter as I walked in.

He wasn't one of those franchisees that trusted everything to managers and assistant managers. He had to be there every second of every minute of every day breathing his hot garlic breath down everyone's neck.

I let myself in through the employee gate and saw Nicholas

back by the fry machine ignoring its alarm while he twirled his baton. Nicholas is the only male baton twirler I know. He's pretty good, I have to admit. But my school is the Highland Scots and the sight of Nicholas in his kilt twirling that baton, well, let's just say it's a good thing he's into spray-on tan.

He immediately dropped the baton and punched the alarm when he saw me.

"Oh, hi Cheyenne," he said, getting all busy with the fries even though they were pretty much burned.

"Hi Nicholas. Where's my dad?"

"Oh, he called and said he'd be a little late, he said I was in charge," Nicholas smiled proudly. "Until you got here, that is."

I walked over to the time clock and noticed Eric talking on his cell. He didn't notice me.

Nicholas blocked my view.

"So, Cheyenne," his voice got deep all of a sudden. "Are you going to the prom?"

There was a knock at the back door and I turned to go.

"Wait a minute," he grabbed my arm. "So are you?"

"Am I what?" I shook his arm off me.

"Going to the prom," he looked at me kind of weird.

"Yeah, like someone would actually ask me." I started to head to the back again but Eric was already at the door, trying to open it.

"So anyway, I was wondering--" Nicholas muttered behind me as I rushed over to Eric.

"How do you get this thing open, Cheyenne?" Eric snarled, but my name sounded like music coming from his lips.

"Let me--" I moved in close to the deadbolt when the door flew open.

It was a tall stack of cardboard boxes and somewhere behind the stack was my dad.

"How many times do I gotta tell you guys, it's two twists to the right, one twist to the left, half a twist to the middle?" he complained then pushed the boxes in through the door on a dolly. As he stepped into the light of the backroom, I could see that his skin was orange, almost as if he had been messing around with some of Nicholas' cream, only there was no trace of lotion. His pale lips contrasted strangely with his skin and his eyes were bloodshot. Around his arm was a large, blood-soaked Band-Aid from where the cow bit him.

"Daddy," I touched the wound. "Didn't you get that checked out yet? It could get infected."

"I'm fine," he muttered.

"What happened Mr. M?" Eric asked.

"Nevermind," Dad said. "Don't just stand there, open the freezer."

Eric ran over to the freezer and opened the door wide as Dad pushed the dolly full of boxes inside.

"What's all that?" I nodded toward the boxes.

"New meat shipment," Dad grunted. "Nicholas!"

"Wait a minute--" I thought about our road kill adventure of the night before. "You're actually gonna put that inside buns and sell it?"

"What'd you think I was gonna do with it? Mulch my roses?"

Eric was already taking the boxes off the dolly.

"I don't know, I thought you'd at least try it out first."

"Try out what?" Nicholas came walking up behind me and made me jump. He grabbed my shoulders, a little too hard, a little too long. "Sorry, didn't mean to scare you, Cheyenne."

I would have shaken him off again but the minute he saw my dad's look, he took his hands off me. I thought I saw Eric smirk, but I couldn't be sure.

"Get in there and start helping Eric unload those boxes," Dad leaned back, groaning. "My back's killing me."

I was about to head back out front to man the counter but Dad pulled my sleeve. He nodded toward his "office," just a nook between the freezer and the bathroom where he'd managed to shove a messy desk. He sat down on it and motioned for me to sit in his chair.

"What's up?" I asked.

It was a great honor to be asked to sit down at work. Coffee break was not in my dad's vocabulary.

He took a ring of keys out of his shirt pocket, held them before me like a hypnotist then took my hand and dropped them into my palm.

I stared at the keys.

"You want me to lock up tonight?" I asked.

"I'm not just asking you to lock up, I'm entrusting you with the keys," he said importantly, like he was giving me the ring of the Lords.

"Okay, cool," I said and was about to shove them in my apron but my dad pressed me back down into the chair gently with two fingers.

"No, no, no," he clucked his tongue. "You don't understand, with great honor comes great responsibility...someday all of this is going to be yours and you gotta know what to do with it."

I stammered speechless. The part about this being mine one day threw me. I never had thought about it like that before. Me, a hamburger heiress.

"Don't worry, Dad, I close with you all the time," I tried to reassure him. "And by the way, Sheila told me to tell you she can't work tonight…uh, her uncle died."

"That girl's got a lot of sick uncles," he chuckled. "I ought to let her go but she's all the eye candy we got."

He must have heard the sigh that came out of me because he got down on his knees and took my chin in his hands.

"Oh honey, I didn't mean it that way, you know you're cute as a button…"

Nicholas walked up, clearing his throat, holding a box of meat.

"This one won't fit, what you want I should do with it," he stared at me instead of my dad.

"Here, gimme that," Dad snatched the box. "Think I'll fry a couple of these puppies up at home…in fact, if you guys wanna make yourselves burgers tonight, go ahead…it's on me!"

"Gee thanks, Merle," Nicholas said.

"Well don't just stand there," my dad said. "Don't you have some lotion to rub on yourself or something?"

Nicholas just cleared his throat some more and took off.

"Now don't close early and don't forget to lock the doors, got it?" Dad turned back to me. "And remember…"

"I know, I know, it's two twists to the right, one twist to the left, half a twist to the middle," I laughed and followed him to the back door and tried to make the key work like it's magic, but no luck.

"Aw, never mind, you shouldn't have to open it tonight, anyway," he said, unlocking it himself. "You kids have fun, now."

As the door slammed behind him, Nicholas pumped his fist and hooted, "Free burgers, yee-haw!"

He jogged into the freezer, reappeared with a box of the mystery meat and sauntered over to Eric at the grill.

"Let's fire one of these puppies up!" Nicholas barked.

"Whatever…" Eric walked away with his cellphone to his ear.

Undaunted, Nicholas ignited the flame under the grill.

"Uh, Nick," I said. "I don't know how excited I would get about that meat, you see my dad--"

As he dug a handful of patties out of the box, I lost my train of thought as I stared at the huge patties. The bloody meat was coarse and fleshy, with sharp tendrils sticking out on all sides. Repulsed as I was, I just couldn't take my eyes off them for what seemed like five whole minutes. Then I thought I saw one of the little tendrils move.

I gasped.

"Yeah, ain't they awesome?" Nicholas said, as he dropped one on the already-hot grill.

The flames leapt up around it and the patty seemed to immediately stretch and unfurl, becoming even larger than the puny bun that was waiting for it. And as I stood watching the meat darken and ooze, it almost seemed to come alive.

"I wonder where he found this stuff," Eric muttered as he walked past.

"I don't know, "Nicholas replied. "But it sure smells great."

THREE

I stood transfixed by the swirling, dancing display of the flaming burgers but something broke me out of my reverie.

"Can I get some service out here?" I heard a shaky voice call out from the counter area.

I peered through the service window to the counter area. There must have been six people lined up! More than we've had in a month!

I rushed toward the register and tugged at Nicholas' sleeve on the way.

"Dude, we've got a dinner rush!" I exclaimed.

"I'm on it!" he said, tugging on my sleeve, arm and shoulder in return.

"Eric!" I yelled. "Slap a dozen more patties on the grill."

From somewhere behind me I could hear him mutter, "Okay, boss..."

I headed for my register and saw a horrific sight. A mom whose belly was so big if her kids stood underneath her she would lose them. If I ever get that fat, I've told several people to shoot me and I'm sure they would, my mother included.

This lady had it under control, though, because her little kids were so busy pinching her fat legs there would be no way she would lose them.

"Welcome to Monster Burger, may I help you?" I said in my most polite voice.

Dad had taught me that. The ruder you think the customer's going to be, the more saccharine you have to sound.

"Yeah, gimme two kid meals," the mom croaked.

"I'm sorry, we don't have 'kids' meals'," I said in my Angelina Jolie-save-the-children voice making sure to flex two fingers around the euphemism 'kids' meals." (Don't kids eat the same food as the rest of us?)

"You mean they don't get no toy?" the mom barked, incensed at the injustice of it all.

"We can cut a Monster Major in half, but…," I wanted to let her down slow. Her kids would be receiving no toy that night. Not from us, anyway.

"Oh," the mother's wide mouth turned into a little, tiny "o", but from below her rose a wailing sound.

"BUT MOMMY, I WANNA TOY!!!"

The mother smacked the creature making noise down below the counter and I could hear it, like a sharp clap in an R&B song. I would have been able to live with witnessing the abuse, but then I heard the mother say, "Shut up! You're gonna split a burger with your brother!!!"

Then sweetly, as nothing violent or barbaric had ever happened, the grotesque woman turned her gaze back to me and said, "And I'll have the salad and an extra-large order of onion rings…oh and a coke, diet, extra ice."

I hadn't been writing all of this down but then I grinned,

gritted my teeth and tried to write down everything in case I would have to recite it for the Child Protective Services agents I planned to call later that night.

As I stuck the order up, I tried to catch Eric's eyes, but he was too busy frying burgers, so I turned to see how Nicholas was faring at the register next to me.

"Welcome to Monster Burger, may I take your order?" I had to hand it to Nicholas; he had trained well and followed all my father's instructions to the tee at all times.

"Ya got coffee?" the ancient old man and woman were back, this time the old man was doing the talking.

"Aw, I don't know...it's probably from this morning...," Nicholas said--too apologetically.

"I'll have one cup of coffee, please," the old man said, hitching up his trousers.

"Uh, is that it sir?" Nicholas asked.

I realized he had about as much training on register as Eric, but he had never asked for a lesson quite as sexily as his co-worker.

"I'll have a hot cup of tea," the little old lady piped up.

"Uh…I think we only have iced tea," Nicholas stammered. I could tell from the way he was looking at the register he was getting confused.

But the old lady didn't care. She sniffed the air.

"Why, that is the most heavenly smell…I think I will have a burger," she said with a euphoric smile on her face.

"Now honey muffin," her husband cut in. "You know beef always gives you gas…"

But Grandma would hear nothing of it.

"Aw, come on, live a little!" she said, raising a gnarled finger. "I'll even take one of those Mondo Monster thingies!"

"Honey muffin!" her husband said in shock.

"Make that two!" she squawked with an impish smile.

I glanced back at the grill and saw Eric holding two spatulas, trying to do double duty. As the flames grew higher, the meat seemed to come alive as the tendrils expanded and contracted in the licking flames.

I almost felt sorry for Eric, watching him work as fast as he could to slap each patty into a bun, slather it with mayo, ketchup and mustard, toss on some vegetables and then top it with a bun.

I say I almost felt sorry for him, if I hadn't been so turned on.

"Number 46!" I yelled, grabbing my order. (It had been so long since we'd had to yell numbers I was still finding my voice.)

The whale-like mother waddled up to the tray with her two urchins in tow.

"Forty-seven!" I could hear Nicholas right behind me, trying to out-do me with his baritone.

A pair of gnarled, shrunken hands latched onto his tray. The little old lady and man walked away with their feast.

I got ready to set my next tray down but then two beefy hands I already recognized grabbed it and I tried to yank it back.

Dirk and Josh were back.

"You aren't number 48!" I spat.

"We are now, Moo Cow," Dirk said with that annoying smile.

I went ahead and let Dirk have the order. It wasn't worth the fight.

Besides, this was the busiest Friday night we'd had since I was 10.

I glanced around the dining room.

The mother shoved onion rings into her mouth, ignoring her salad, while her little girl wrapped her mouth around half her burger and bit down, chewing with the sound of kindling snapping.

Meanwhile, her brother masticated in lethargic ecstasy, eyes half-closed.

I glanced over to another table where two policemen ripped chunks out of their burgers with bared teeth.

My eyes went back to the little old lady who was chomping like a horse, her false teeth clacking like hooves on the pavement. Across from me, her husband tore into his burger, panting and grunting between bites.

"What's wrong with everybody?" I thought, half aloud. Even I would have killed for a Monster Burger at that point after having no dinner, but I certainly wouldn't behave like some wolf over freshly-killed carrion.

Suddenly, when an urge to shove a fistful of Cheez-its into my face bubbled up to my stomach, I stomped over to the salad bar and snatched a bit of celery.

I dipped it into the ranch dressing as far as it would go then shoved it into my mouth, taking angry bites. At one point my mother had hooked me up with this guy called a "food counselor" and I guess this is what he would have called "anger eating" but to hell with him. I'd like to hear him say that the next time I'm sitting next to a big, heavy watermelon....

At that moment I felt something bounce off my face. I looked down at the floor and saw a radish rolling by.

I looked over across the sneeze-guard and saw Dirk there smiling at me, half his burger in his hand--the other half in his cheek.

It took every fiber in my body not to scoop up the ceramic canisters and start lobbing globs of Jell-O, pasta salad and miniature corn at his lame ass but then I heard a voice.

"Uh, Cheyenne--" it was Nicholas.

I turned to see him about six deep in customers.

"Do you think you could tell Eric to throw some more patties on the grill?" he asked.

I turned back to the grill area and had to swallow hard to stifle my reaction. Eric was making out with Destiny Fines, this cheerleader chick who has been laughing at me since fifth grade but who has since decided she is all Gidge-Goth with pink and black strands in her Barbie-blonde hair. She's been into leather and piercing too, but I can tell it's all fake. Even if it's real, it's fake.

I try to act like Dirty Harry's girlfriend and stomp back to the backroom but I'm not as good as my dad at 70's B-movie drama.

"You gotta do something about your friend, Eric," I said, not even caring that they were still making out.

But Eric seemed to care because he extricated himself from Destiny's grasp--all embarrassed.

"Sorry, Cheyenne--" he said and it was impossible to tell if he meant sorry I'm not with you or sorry I'm such a general asshole.

"Uh, I'm his *girlfriend*," Destiny said snottily.

"I'm talking about Dirk," I interrupted. "He's out there with Josh making a mess..."

Eric ducked out of Destiny's grasp, "Okay, keep an eye on those burgers, wouldya Cheyenne? I gotta get a new box."

Eric ducked all responsibility by ducking into the freezer.

"Oh, and next time, use the customer entrance, okay, Destiny?" I said, this time, not caring if I sounded like a bitch.

"Did they already have a uniform with an ass that big or did you have it custom made?" Destiny shot back.

Eric came out of the freezer and shoved the box of meat at me before I could tell Destiny what I thought about my ass. Meanwhile, she flipped her pink-black-blonde hair and followed Eric to the front. Once a cheerleader, always a cheerleader.

I followed both of them and saw that Nicholas' six-deep line had turned into a twelve-deep line. I couldn't believe it. There hadn't been this many people inside Monster Burger since the Highland Highlanders had won Homecoming six years ago and even then most of them had just asked for cups of water. These people were handing over cold, hard fists of cash. My dad was gonna freak.

But then I looked over by the soda machine.

Dirk was back and so was his friend Josh. They were squirting ketchup at each other, taking bites of Monster Burgers with their free hands.

I was going to go over to them and tell them to knock it off, but I was surprised when Eric beat me to it.

"Knock it off you guys," he said.

"What? They're just having a little fun," his smarmy cheerleader girlfriend said.

Was it just me or did her eyes flash over Dirk's butt?

"A little fun?" Eric said. "This is where I work, Destiny..."

Dirk suddenly tossed the ketchup onto a nearby table.

"Come on, you ready to blow, Destiny?"

I tried to pretend I was wiping the counter down but I wanted to hear this. Was Dirk trying to steal Destiny back from Eric? They had gone out together a long time ago--like the beginning of the school year, but I didn't think either of them still had feelings.

"Are you stepping out on me?" Eric said in an accusing tone. Evidently I wasn't the only one who had picked up on the adulterous vibes.

"Oh, honey bunny," she said sickeningly, squeezing Eric's cheeks between her fingers. "I said I'd drive those two losers to the game..."

"Are you going back on the cheerleading squad?" Eric said, outraged. "I thought you said football was gay..."

"Oh and you wearing eyeliner and pretending to be a rock star isn't?" she tittered in that same voice she had used on me all those years ago.

Eric started to walk away but Destiny grabbed his collar and brought his face towards hers. Did she actually expect a kiss after all that?

"Relax, I'll come pick you up after you get off," she said.

He didn't respond to her lips because something had caught his eye across the room.

"What time do you want me to come by, babe?" Destiny said, oblivious to whatever he was looking at.

"Huh?" Eric looked like he was watching a slow-motion car wreck. "I'll call you. I don't know if I'm going to feel like partying tonight--things are kind of crazy right now..."

I looked in the same direction as Eric and saw the craziness.

The fat lady's daughter projectile-vomited all over her brother who had just jet-barfed all over my dad's Monster Burger cut-out.

I heard choking from another table and turned my head just in time to see the little old lady groaning and holding her sides as she made her way to the exit followed by her old man dry-heaving behind her.

Eric stepped out from the counter and looked all around at

the mess.

"Would you look at this?" he said.

"Yeah..." I echoed.

"Nicholas!" he barked, sounding almost like my dad. "Get out here."

His blue eyes somehow got a lot paler right at that moment.

It didn't matter, though, because Destiny was still right behind him.

"*Eeew*," she squealed. "This place is totally gross...I don't see how you can work here."

She started to head for the front door. I thought Eric was actually going to follow her until he bumped into Nicholas.

"You wanted me?" Eric asked.

"Yeah," Eric said. "Get a mop and bucket and clean up this mess..."

He looked after Destiny and called to her, "I'll call you after I'm through!"

I turned away from the horrid scene and ran to the back.

"Cheyenne, wait!" Eric called.

I never thought I'd hear his voice and want to get away from it.

I ran past the grill, the freezer and the bathroom, back to my dad's little "office." I picked up his old-fashioned rotary phone and started to dial his cell number. (It was so old I was the only one there who knew how to use it.)

Eric appeared in the archway to my dad's little hovel.

"Cheyenne, what are you doing?" he asked.

I would have liked to have told him I'm digging my heart out for you, I'm laying twisted upon the rock upon the shore for your love but I'm not that poetic and all I could think to say was, "I'm calling my dad."

FOUR

The three of us argued back and forth for a while. Girls against boys. Nicholas and Eric both seemed to think that if we called my dad he might somehow pin the whole mess on us and take the damages out of our pay.

I finally had to admit they were right. It was exactly the cheap-ass type of thing my dad might do but somewhere in the back of my mind I liked to think he might be concerned that his little girl was surrounded by a bunch of vomiting, red-faced freaks.

Then I suggested that if we weren't going to call my dad we at least had to hide the evidence. I grabbed two mops and shoved them toward my underlings.

"I ain't cleaning that shit up," Eric snorted folding his arms with a flip of his lovable locks.

"I've *done* my part," Nicholas pushed the mop away.

"It's not about doing your part, it's about keeping your job," I snapped.

I suddenly felt I was being watched. I turned around slowly and saw one of the policemen standing there. He was built like a redwood tree but that wasn't what threw me. No, he looked like a *red* redwood tree, with skin the color of an almost ripe tomato, and pale orange lips. Hell, even the whites of his eyes were red. And what eyes. They bore through me with a tombstone stare.

"Shit, we're in trouble," Eric whispered behind me.

"Yeah, he's probably going to shut us down," Nicholas murmured.

I jumped as the cop slammed his hand down hard on the counter.

"Meat." It wasn't so much a word as a sound.

I smoothed my apron with quivering hands and stepped up to the counter.

"Yeah, we're really sorry, about all the sick people, officer, we got this new shipment of meat today and--"

"NEED MEAT!" he lunged toward me over the counter.

"Well don't just stand there dilweed, get the officer a burger," it was Nicholas' turn to bark at Eric.

Eric ducked back to the grill as Nicholas and I watched the cop sway uncertainly on his feet, foam bubbling at the corner of his mouth. The cop watched us with that same unwavering stare.

"Uh, can I get you a drink with that?" I asked, as much to cover the sound of the cop's wheezy breathing as to get his order.

But Iron Lung just exhaled some more and stared at me.

I whirled away quickly to get a soda cup. I peeked through the service window where Eric was in a mesmerized trance, watching the raw meat on the grill sizzle and expand.

"Can't you turn up the heat on that?"

"It's coming!"

Just then Eric did the unthinkable. He took out his cellphone and dialed. I knew who he was calling. I wanted to reach through the window, grab that phone and throw it on the burner.

But all I did was whirl back around to the monster cop and set the cup down on the counter

"That'll be four seventy-nine, please."

The cop stared at me with red, dead eyes.

I hit void and opened the cash drawer, "On second thought, let's make it on the house."

Finally, a wrapped burger appeared on the service window ledge as Eric called out, "Order up!"

I set the burger on the tray and placed it before the cop.

The cop looked at the burger with fire in his blood-shot eyes, then leaned over and tore through the wrapper with his teeth, feeding on the burger like a wolf over a carcass.

I took a step back and bumped into Nicholas. We both stared in horror.

The cop looked up with a mouthful of bloody meat, a trace of a smile on his lips.

I picked up a rag and let myself into the dining area, taking care to cut a wide circle around the chomping cop.

"What are you doing?" Nicholas called.

"Someone's gotta clean up this mess," I shot back.

I worked my rag against the Formica tabletop, swallowing hard to hold back the bile rising in my throat.

All of a sudden, the fat lady with the obnoxious kids burst through the front door--only her kids weren't with her. I watched her push through the double doors into the kiddie area. She headed straight toward the ball pit where

her daughter rose up out of the rainbow-colored spheres like some kind of Romper Room vampire. The kid's skin was dull red, her mouth bubbled with foam. Then even creepier, her brother rose up behind her--face the color of a tomato.

"Where have you been?" The mother cried. "I been looking all over for you two! Come here this instant!!"

Lacy and Tyler made no effort to go toward their mother and only continued to teeter in the multi-colored balls, groaning.

The mother made her big mistake when she took a step toward her daughter.

"Why are you so red? You been playing with yourself again?"

Almost as if in response to the tactless comment, the little girl stepped toward her mother, grabbed her hand and bit into it.

"Lacey!!" the mother withdrew her hand, screaming in pain. "What are you doing?"

But it was no use, her son had latched onto her other arm.

"No, stop!"

But the kids continued their feeding frenzy as their mother sank down into the balls.

I watched all this frozen, as if in a dream. Then just

as the children finished their feeding I realized what I must do. I grabbed a chair, ran to the double doors and lodged the chair underneath. That would hold them for a little while.

I ran back to the dining room where the cop was just finishing up his burger.

He stood up from the table, swaying and breathing heavily. I ran up behind him and tapped him on the shoulder.

"Excuse me," I said.

The cop turned around, eyes blazing, skin red.

He grabbed my arm.

I tried to pull free, but the big lunk pulled my arm up to his mouth. He curled back his lips to reveal long white teeth, waiting to bite.

"Let me go!!!"

I pulled, but it was no use. That cop was going to make dessert out of my arm, no matter what. But just then, he turned me loose.

I felt a warm sensation go whizzing past my nose.

I looked back at the cop who covered his face with his hands while smoking grease oozed from his fingers.

Nicholas stood there, holding a pan dripping with grease. We both watched as the cop's face turned brown and started to sizzle and expand, like the patties on the grill.

The cop's body seems to grow in size and proportion.

His red eyes danced like coals on a fire.

I stood mesmerized by those glowing embers until Nicholas grabbed my hand and dragged me to the backroom.

Eric was on his cell phone, typical.

"Eric! Call the cops!" I cried.

"Uh, that was a cop," Nicholas muttered. He opened the freezer door. "Quick, in here, Cheyenne!"

"Eric, get off the phone!" I screamed.

I grabbed Eric's arm and dragged him toward the freezer.

On the way, I caught a glimpse of the cop, face brown and sizzling, busting through the employee gate.

I dragged Eric in as Nicholas shut the door behind us.

"Call the cops," Nicholas said.

I couldn't believe after all this time, that Eric had his

cellphone glued to his ear.

"I'm trying to call Destiny..." he waved us away with his

hand.

As if we were just in a mall food court and not stuck in a

freezer with a mad-cow cop about to break down the door.

"Would you forget about Destiny for a minute and call the

cops?"

"What for?" Eric finally pulled his ear away from his phone.

"That cop out there attacked Cheyenne."

"No way," Eric obviously had been somewhere else for the

past twenty minutes.

"It's like they've got a sickness or something. It's gotta be the

meat..."

Eric handed his phone to me.

"You call 'em. I don't wanna sound like a loony."

I took the phone and dialed 911.

All I heard was a recording: "Due to the high volume of calls, your call will be answered in the order it was received..."

FIVE

We sat around in the freezer for about two more minutes looking at each other when finally Eric ripped the phone out of my hands and speed-dialed Destiny.

"Hello?" we heard Destiny's raspy, weak voice come through the speaker.

"Destiny, it's me, I've been trying to call you for the last hour--"

"Oh God, it hurts so bad."

"What hurts?"

"You're right, Dirk is an asshole...I gotta go--"

There was a thud, then static crackled through the phone line.

"Destiny...wait, where are you?"

Another voice came on the line. It sounded like Dirk's voice, dropped a thousand octaves and filled with evil.

"Need meat!"

Another thud, then slow, thundering footsteps.

"Dirk, is that you?...damn!"

Eric slammed shut his phone then turned toward the door.

Nicholas blocked his path.

"Don't open the door, dude."

"Get outta my way..."

"That cop is out there..."

"Yeah, and who knows how many other..." I muttered.

"How many other what?"

"Don't you get it, Eric? Everyone who ate that meat, they're all going crazy!"

Eric's eyes bulged.

"Look, Eric, just stay here," I tried to calm him down. "I'm sure Destiny's fine."

Eric looked at me then hit the big button on the wall. The door opened.

The cop stood in the doorway, skin still sizzling, teeth like fangs.

Eric grabbed a can of pickles and threw it at the cop. The can made a sickening squelch as it hit the cop's skull, like teeth sinking into a pickle. The cop stumbled, and Eric ducked out.

"Shut the door, Nicholas!"

Nicholas tried to shut the door, but the cop already had one foot in the freezer.

He grabbed Nicholas by the shoulders and started to bite, but Nicholas ducked away at the last second. The cop tumbled inside the freezer, as an avalanche of boxes tumbled onto his head.

"Cheyenne, come on!"

I ran out of the freezer and watched as Nicholas slammed the door shut, locking the cop into the icy cold.

"Where's Eric?" I looked around.

"Probably getting himself killed," Nicholas nodded toward

the service window. "Get away from there, you don't want them to see you."

"You think there's more of them?"

I turned and stared through the opening and saw a sea of red-faced people stumbling forward, their low noises reminded me of a swarm of bees.

Eric stood in front of Freezer Man's partner, thrusting a mop like it was a medieval sword. The cop bit into the wooden handle and chewed discontentedly.

Eric dropped the mop and backed up. The cop stumbled closer to him, cornering him against the salad bar.

I turned and grabbed a knife from above the grill.

"What the hell are you doing?" Nicholas snorted.

"I can't just let him stay out there and die."

I started toward the employee gate to the dining area but Nicholas blocked my way. He put his orange hands against the wall behind me, trapping me between his arms.

"He doesn't give a shit about you, you know."

"Let me go, Nicholas..."

"Who says 'hello Cheyenne' every time you come on shift?"

I heard Eric's muffled yells and took a step forward, but Nicholas wasn't gonna move his skinny yellow arms.

"Who asked you to the prom?"

"You didn't ask me to the prom!"

"I asked you if you were going..."

"There's a difference--"

I heard sounds of a struggle from the front. Was that Eric choking?

"Are you gonna let me go?"

"Who lays awake every night thinking about you?"

"You lay awake every night thinking about me?"

Nicholas leaned forward looking deep into my eyes, like he was about to move in for the kiss.

With his large, blue eyes so close to mine, something came

over me. Suddenly I forgot about his orange-tinged skin, his mouth breathing, his dumb jokes...there was something going on here and I wasn't sure what it was.

Then I heard the magic words.

"Cheyenne!!!" it was Eric's helpless cry.

I pushed Nicholas out of the way and rushed through the employee gate.

"Cheyenne!" Nicholas called after me.

"God...what!" I snapped and turned back around to see him holding a large carving knife.

"I've got your back," he said with a smile.

I had to smile back before I rushed out to the dining room.

A red-faced customer had Eric by the shoulders, baring its teeth, preparing to bite into him.

I charged forward with my knife, not knowing exactly what to do. I stopped short.

I'd never stabbed anyone before. Hell, I'd never even hit anyone before but after this I resolved to give Destiny Fines one hell of a bitch slap.

The customer groaned and leaned towards Eric's neck. I let him have it, right in the brain with the knife.

The thing dropped face forward onto Eric's back. Eric moved away and the customer slithered to the ground--dead, I hoped.

Nicholas came running out, knife ready, but he lowered it when he saw the dead customer.

"Damn, Cheyenne, you've got balls."

Eric whipped out his cell phone and started dialing.

"Yeah, thanks Cheyenne."

I rolled my eyes and started to turn away, but another customer was already coming up behind him.

"Eric, behind you!"

I picked up the mop and bashed the thing between the eyes with it.

It stumbled backward. Nicholas finished the thing off, plunging his knife right between its eyes with a bloody spurt.

"Come on, let's get in the back," I pulled Eric's sleeve.

"Are you kidding? I'm gonna get the hell out of here!"

"How?"

I nodded toward the front window where dozens of customers were wandering through the parking lot, growling. Suddenly I thought of Sheila. Was she out there battling? Or had she become one of them?

"We can take 'em." Eric's words interrupted my dark reverie.

"No we can't," I protested.

Eric reached down and started to pull the knife out of the customer's head, but the creature leapt to life and wrapped itself around Eric's legs.

Eric screamed and fell to the floor in terror. Without thinking this time, I kicked the miserable thing in the head as Nicholas pulled Eric out of its grasp.

Eric leaned on Nicholas as he headed for the back and I couldn't help thinking how weak my crush suddenly looked in the arms of someone I once thought so nerdy.

As we got to the backroom, Nicholas ran into the bathroom and slammed the door, leaving me and Eric to stand helplessly and awkwardly outside as the red-faced throng made their slow push toward the employee gate.

SIX

As I slumped against the wall, my mind went blank.

I wanted to go grab more knives from over the grill, but the service window was clogged with waving red arms, like some kind of human anemone.

I wanted to ask Nicholas what to do but he was still locked in the bathroom and the only other person I could turn to was at the back door, frantically and futilely fiddling with the deadbolt.

I walked over, pushed Eric out of the way and tried my hand at it, but I couldn't remember if it was two twists to the right or two twists to the left.

He elbowed me, "C'mon, Cheyenne, I almost had it—"

The unmistakable sound of barfing came from the other side of the wall.

Eric jumped away from the door, "What was that?"

"Probably just….Nicholas—"

We turned around and he was standing there, wiping his mouth, skin a faint orange.

"He's turning orange—just like one of…them!" Eric pointed accusingly.

"It's just his tanning spray—"

"No, it's these stupid zit pills," Nicholas produced a small bottle from his shirt pocket. "They always make me puke." He stared at us, incredulously. "What'd you think, I'm turning into some kind of freaking zombie?"

Nicholas stomped over to the freezer and opened the door. I cried out for him to stop, but inside the cop laid motionless with his head against a case of salad dressing, head frosted over like a month-old carton of ice cream.

Nicholas stepped inside the freezer, lifted the cop's arm and let it drop.

"Is he dead?"

"No, just frozen. Like the patties. They only plump when we cook 'em."

"You're right," Eric said. "There was something hella weird about that meat --whenever I put one on the grill it was like it was alive or something."

"Uh, it was alive," it was my turn to roll my eyes. "Duh, it used to be a cow."

"Well, while you two are arguing about the life cycle of a cow, what are we going to do about them?" Eric nodded toward the employee gate. The sheer force of bodies had taken the door off its hinges and now the nice little old lady stood glowering in the doorway, chewing her own bottom lip into a bloody pulp.

"Oh, my God, what are we going to do?"

"Simple, my dear," Nicholas waved his hand with a flourish toward the open freezer. "Just shove them into the icebox!"

It wasn't so hard once we got started. The old lady was an easy push; I just had to make sure she didn't bite my hand. Her husband was a little harder. He wanted to grab onto my arm, but Eric got behind me with the frying pan and bashed him on the head. It stunned him enough for Nicholas and me to drag him the rest of the way inside.

The cop's partner was a tougher sell, but once Eric banged him a few dozen times with the pan and I stuck a spoon down his throat, in he went. In between Nicholas would shut the door and lock it. It only took a few seconds for them to settle down inside and succumb to the cold.

The trouble was, it started getting crowded in there.

"I don't think I can fit many more in," Nicholas said as he shut the door on a flailing red arm.

"We've got to!" I cried as Eric banged a trucker in the nose with the pan. "We don't have anywhere else for them to go."

"Even if we could fit them, I think with all the bodies in there, it could start to make the temperature rise."

"Great, just turn down the thermostat!" Eric said, helping me push the trucker toward the door.

"Yeah, but there's just one problem," Nicholas said, giving the trucker a quick kick which sent him sprawling on top of the other frozen bodies. "The thermostat is inside the freezer."

We stood there pondering this for a moment, even as our next "customer" staggered toward us.

Suddenly I heard the phone ring.

I ran from our assembly line back to the messy desk my dad keeps in the far corner of the backroom.

"Hey, Cheyenne!" I could hear Eric calling after me.

When I got to the desk, I could barely find the phone underneath a messy stack of

papers.

"Monster Burger, may I help you?" it was a dumb way to answer the phone

during an apocalypse, but old habits die hard.

I waited for a reply but all I could hear was air whistling into the receiver on the other end.

"Hello, is anybody there?"

I turned around and looked back toward the freezer. Eric was holding his own against two freaks.

"Hello?" Still nothing.

I slammed down the phone and ran back to the freezer where Nicholas strained to shut the door on half a dozen waving red, bleeding arms while Eric swatted at them with the pan. Finally he got the door shut tight. Thank God it locked from the outside.

But more of them stumbled through the employee gate. I picked up a pot lid and started banging customers in the head.

"Where are they all coming from?" Eric cried as he double-slammed with his frying pan.

"Yeah, there's no way this many people ate here tonight!" Nicholas added.

"Look at their arms," I nodded toward the flailing appendages coming out of the freezer. "They look like they've been gnawed on by werewolves."

"That's crazy! Who ever heard of food poisoning spread by bites?" Eric retorted, chipping the tooth of a middle aged woman with dead eyes.

"Uh, dude, I hate to tell you this, but the Hanta virus was spread by rat bites," Nicholas leaned with all his weight against the freezer door.

"And don't forget the Bubonic plague...," I said, running over to put my considerable weight against the door.

I could feel it give a few inches.

"Well, that's ridiculous; there aren't any rats in here!" Eric put his pan down, as if to make a point.

Suddenly the freezer door burst open. I went face first into the wall as cold red bodies ran past me.

"Cheyenne!" I could feel hands on me, warm hands. It was Nicholas.

He pulled me behind a stack of five-gallon buckets.

I watched in horror as Eric swung his pan wildly, hitting one then another customer in the head. But soon they were coming so fast he didn't have time to make a full swing, so he just agitated the pan frantically, like a kid playing with a paddle ball.

Somehow, he held his own. Either the customers wandered off in dumb pain or steered clear of the gyrating piece of cast iron. He yelled as he fought and from his shaking arm, I could tell he couldn't hold the heavy cookware up in the air much longer.

And then through the throng one more "customer" appeared, the worst one we'd ever had: Dirk.

I grabbed one of the buckets.

"What the hell are you doing?" Nicholas whispered.

"What do you think I'm going to do? I'm gonna pound that asshole into the ground!"

But as I went to the lift the bucket, it was heavier than I thought. I glanced down at the label. Lard. Seventy-five pounds of it.

Dirk stood in front of Eric, face smeared with blood and skin as red as the devil.

Eric raised his pan high in the air.

"Oh, you don't know how long I've been waiting to do this, bro'....yeah, who's the tough man now, Dirk the Dick!"

Dirk moaned, and then batted the pan out of Eric's hand.

Eric took a step back.

I roared and heaved the bucket up to my chest, then with one more burst of energy, I raised it up over my head.

I ran toward Dirk, carried by the weight of my burden, then I gave every last ounce of energy I had as I smacked the bucket into Dirk's head.

Dirk's head bent sideways, then I let go of the bucket. It and Dirk dropped to the floor.

The lard spilled out onto Dirk's twisted neck.

"Yes!" I looked over to Eric who was smiling from ear-to-ear, blue eyes twinkling.

What I would have given for that smile a few hours earlier. But at that moment, all I wanted to do was throw up.

SEVEN

The throng of customers seemed to have temporarily eased off.

Either we had already hit enough of them in the head and shoved them in the freezer, or they had moved onto other sources of nourishment. Red Devil Pizza down the road. Or maybe they were after the swankier flesh at the Morgan's Steakhouse off Highway 6.

I wiped some blood from my cheek and headed toward the sink. I was thirsty, I was tired and for some strange reason I was hungry.

I put my mouth under the faucet and let the cool water rush into my mouth and over my face, washing away the blood flecks and sweat accumulated during who knows how many hours of fighting off stiff, dead human beings intent on only one thing.

I turned off the water and stood up, wiping my mouth.

Standing there in the doorway of the back room was another bloody, red-faced dead-eyed non-human. Only this one I recognized for even in death, she couldn't lose the snide upturn of the left side of her mouth. Destiny.

She looked like hell, literally, with the bottom half of her right arm thrashed to a pulpy mess as though she had been chewed on by a pack of rabid dogs.

"Destiny!"

Eric, who had been slumped against the wall, suddenly sprang to attention.

"No, stay there!" I called to him.

He ignored me and rushed over, but when he got within a foot of her he stopped and stared.

"My, God, babe, what happened to your arm?"

Destiny leaned forward, reached out toward him. I spied a fire extinguisher in the corner, and picked it up.

Just as Eric reached out to take her hand, I clocked her in the head. Her eyes rolled back under her eyelids and she stumbled sideways.

Eric went to catch her, "Shit, Cheyenne. What'd you do that for?"

"She wants to eat you," I said, batting Destiny to the ground with the butt of the extinguisher.

"No, she doesn't!"

Eric bent down over and Destiny, who had regained consciousness.

I smashed her in the forehead and she went limp on the floor.

"Would you knock it off?" Eric snarled at me. I could tell he hated me. But I didn't care.

"That's not Destiny, Eric...we've got to get out of here, there's no way we can take on all of these...things."

Eric sobbed over Destiny's unconscious body.

A tear dripped onto Destiny's bloody eyelid. It snapped open like a Venetian blind. Her arms went up around Eric's neck.

He returned her rigor mortis grip with a sweet caress then started to help her up to her feet.

"Ok, babe, that's it...we're gonna get you some help."

The sight of her red arm around his shoulder made me sick. I felt desperate to get her away from him. Even more desperate than I had when she was just a cheerleader.

But then again these were desperate times, and they called for desperate measures.

I ran back to Daddy's desk. I rifled through the cigarette packs and nudie magazines in his desk until I found what I was looking for—his Colt .45. The one he always bragged about having but which I had never seen, except once. It was right after the divorce. Mom had dropped me off for one of my first "Daddy weekends" and I walked into the backroom. He had the gun to his temple. I rushed in right as he was about to pull the trigger.

"Daddy!" I had cried.

He turned around and looked at me with an awkward mixture of guilt and terror. Then he had grinned, "Aw, it's empty pumpkin! Do you think I could ever leave you? Just, playing that little game makes me feel better...somehow."

I opened up the bullet chamber to see if he'd put more bullets in and gasped. The bullet chamber was full except for one empty compartment.

I ran back into the backroom. Eric stroked Destiny's hair as she growled. Suddenly, she bared her teeth and sank them into Eric's neck.

I lifted up the gun and pulled the trigger. Blood spurted from Destiny's eye, splattering all over Eric's face.

As she fell to the floor, lifeless, Eric collapsed on top of her, sobbing.

"Get away from her, Eric, she might not be dead!"

Eric lifted his head from her chest.

"You shot my girlfriend! Why did you do that, Cheyenne? You shot my fucking girlfriend!!!"

"That wasn't your girlfriend, Eric, at least, not anymore."

"Oh, yeah, well that's not your dad either, Cheyenne!"

I felt a hot hand clamp down on my shoulder. I turned around slowly and saw my father.

At least something that used to be my father. His skin was bright red, there was foam at the corner of his mouth and those eyes, well, they were not the eyes of the man who always used to read to me out of his Chevy manual before tucking me into bed at night.

"Daddy?" I leaned forward to touch him but I recoiled after a deep, gravelly growl arose from his throat.

Nicholas pushed in front of me.

"Merle? Hey, boy are we glad to see you—"

Daddy stood there for a moment, then a creepy grin formed on his face.

"Back up, Nicholas," I whispered, pulling Nicholas back just as my dad lunged at us.

"Daddy, no!"

He stopped. For a split second, I almost thought he recognized me, then he jumped toward Nicholas who ran off, pushing past customers to get to the dining area.

I bent down and scrambled around on the floor, looking for the gun I had dropped.

"Looking for this?"

I looked up to see my Uncle Charlie standing there, holding the revolver by the trigger. He himself had a shotgun strapped across his chest.

"Uncle Charlie—my dad, he…," I collapsed sobbing into his arms.

"I know, honey, I never should have helped him butcher that cow—" he patted my back.

"That's right," I pulled away from him. "This is all your fault."

"My fault? How was I supposed to know…"

He looked hurt and angry then his eyes widened as they fixed on something out in the dining area.

"What?"

I pushed past him toward the counter area. Dad had his hands around Nicholas' throat.

"Daddy, no!" I cried. I rushed forward and pummeled his back with useless punches.

Nicholas clawed at Dad's hands, trying to free himself from the chokehold. He was turning blue.

A shot rang out. Daddy's head flew back and his hands dropped from around Nicholas' neck. I turned to see Uncle Charlie standing there with the shotgun.

EIGHT

My dad lay there, his eyes closed, as blood seeped through his shirt, then spilled out of his sleeves onto the floor.

I felt like I had been kicked in the stomach. Like someone had inserted a tube into my lungs and sucked all the air out.

I sunk to my knees. I tried to cry, but all that came out was a weird wheezing sound. I could feel tears stinging my eyes, but they wouldn't come out either. It was like my whole body was shutting down.

Charlie bent his head down to Dad's chest, listening for a heartbeat.

When he lifted his head back up, his lips were set tight. There were tears in his eyes, too, but he was fighting to keep them back.

"He's gone," Charlie said.

"Shit, no," Nicholas said, still rubbing his neck.

"It's ok, if the old Merle saw this place, he'd go into cardiac arrest, anyway."

I suddenly felt the breath come back into my lungs. I got up and shoved Uncle Charlie in the chest.

"You didn't have to shoot him, you son-of-a-bitch!"

Nicholas pulled me back.

"Yes he did, your dad was going to kill me, Cheyenne."

I sunk back down to my knees. Sobbing, I looked around at the broken windows and the customers digging through the trash, feasting away on bodies at the tables. Charlie was right. Monster Burger had gone to hell and it would have killed my dad to see it.

Charlie took a small vial out of his coat pocket. He opened the container and shoved a few pills into my dad's mouth.

93

"C'mon, swallow these, you can do it, buddy."

"What are those?"

"Antibiotics--strong enough for a cow..."

"But I thought you said he was…"

"I don't know, it's worth a try."

A customer, maybe one of our trucker regulars, but it was hard to tell, reached across the counter and dug into the ketchup container. He took his hand out, dripping with ketchup. As he clumsily licked the ketchup, it smeared all over his face.

He looked right at me, eyes red and dead.

"Shoot it Uncle Charlie," I said.

"Now, Cheyenne, I gotta conserve the bullets.."

"I said shoot it, goddammit!"

Charlie handed my gun back to me.

"You do it."

I held the gun up to the customer's face, my hand shaking. Part of me hated to see anymore bloodshed, but another part of me hated these things, these monsters, that had killed my father and destroyed my life. I closed my eyes and squeezed the trigger. True blood and ketchup spattered in all directions as the customer fell to the ground.

I felt the heat of the gun against my skin as I stuck it into the waistband of my khakis.

Other customers, attracted by the commotion, left their feeding and stumbled toward us.

"Okay, let's see if we can make it to the drive-through window, maybe we can crawl out of it," Uncle Charlie said, his voice just above a whisper.

"What about Daddy?" I cried, a little too loudly, the customers quickened their gait.

"I've got him," Charlie bent down and in one fluid movement slung my dad over his shoulder like a sack of potatoes. He started to trudge toward the drive-through.

Outside the window, the cop that had tried to eat my hand was wandering back and forth in a daze.

"Hey, what's he doing out there," I said, half to myself. "I thought we locked him in the—''

My eyes drifted over to the back room. Through the employee gate I could see the freezer door, it was open and except for a bunch of torn boxes, the freezer was completely empty.

"Nicholas, the freezer, they all got out!" I cried.

Nicholas grabbed some stainless steel forks and knives from a dispenser.

"All the more reason for us to get the hell out of here," he said. "I'll be right behind you, okay, on the count of three….1…2…"

"Cheyenne!" I turned to see Eric, neck and face bloody, come limping toward me.

"Come on, forget about him, he's a goner," Nicholas nudged me with a fork.

"Maybe we can help him, just like Uncle Charlie is helping my dad."

I looked toward the drive-through. Uncle Charlie, using Dad as a battering ram, had almost made it.

I turned back around and Eric collapsed onto me, crying. His once beautifully pale skin was now pale orange and his dreamy blue eyes were now burning red. How many times had I dreamed about holding him in my arms, but never like this: helpless and smelling like death.

I slipped one arm under Eric's armpit and kept one hand free to reach for the gun.

I took a step, dragging Eric with me.

"Okay, let's go!" I yelled to Nicholas.

"So help me, if this asshole slows us down, it's gonna be him who gets the fork between the eyes!" Nicholas muttered.

As we made our way to the drive-through window, customers staggered toward us, but stopped short as they came toward Eric. Either they didn't want to eat someone who was almost one of their own or there was a finders keepers rule among them.

When we got to the window, there was no sign of Charlie or my dad.

I turned back towards Nicholas.

"Where'd they go?"

"Who?"

"My dad and my uncle you dolt."

"Maybe they got out before us."

"I don't know," I stared at the drive-through window. It was still closed.

"Come on, Cheyenne, we don't have time to look for them. Let's just get out of here."

"Easier said than done," I nodded toward the window where outside the cop groaned and walked toward the window.

"Great, I guess I'm going to have to use another bullet," I complained, reaching for my waistband.

"I got this," Nicholas said, and before I could stop him, he had leapt out the window with his fork and promptly stabbed it in the cop's eye. Blood spurted as the cop turned in circles, the fork sticking out of his head as if he was some kind of overgrown cocktail meatball.

Nicholas held out his hands and smiled.

"Am I cool or what? Now just jump into my arms…"

I still had Eric clinging to my arm like a possum.

"Okay, I'll try to push him out to you," I called through the window.

"Not him! I meant you," Nicholas barked. "Why don't you just leave him there? He always wanted to work the window."

I gave Nicholas a dirty look then I extricated my arm from Eric's grasp. He groaned and a long string of drool fell from his mouth.

"It's okay, I have a plan," I told him.

I stuck my feet out of the window and was going to jump down by myself, but Nicholas was already there, one hand under my butt, the other perilously close to my breast area.

"What the hell are you doing?" I snapped.

"Helping you—"

"I can get out myself, now put me down!"

"Okay, jeez, Cheyenne, I was just trying to save your life...again!"

I stood on my tiptoes and leaned back in the window. Eric wavered unsteadily as a growling customer eyed him, as if deciding whether he was still good enough to eat.

I reached in and grabbed Eric by the shoulders and pulled him out the window. My plan was to ease him out and lower him down, but I didn't realize that despite his sinewy frame, he weighed way more than I thought. Together we both fell to the ground.

For a moment, as he lay on top of me, I looked into his eyes and thought I detected a human emotion. Was it lust? Gratitude? His face came closer. Even in his altered state, he realized what he had really wanted all along...

Then I felt something sliding on my bare skin, underneath my shirt, down towards my pants. Was that a hand? Was Eric actually trying to…? At that moment I realized it was too smooth and cold to be a hand—even Eric's. The shot that rang out confirmed my suspicion. Eric slumped down on my neck; blood cascaded from a wound at the back of his head.

I rolled out from under him and saw Nicholas standing there with the gun from my dad's desk.

"What did you do?" I cried, not caring that my voice sounded shrill, hysterical.

"He was gonna put the bite on you, Cheyenne."

"No he wasn't!"

I stood up and marched towards him. It took all my restraint not to kick him in the shins.

"Well he sure as hell wasn't going to kiss you."

The hell with restraint. I scrunched up my fist and socked him in the jaw.

Nicholas stumbled backwards and grabbed his face.

"Ow! What was that for?"

"For being an asshole! Give me my gun back!"

"Hell no, you're probably going to shoot me with it."

"That's a chance you're gonna have to take."

Uncle Charlie's unholy scream came from within the restaurant. Nicholas and I both ran back to the drive-through window and peered inside.

Charlie ran toward the window. My dad, groaning and angry, chased close behind.

"Yeah," Nicholas muttered. "I don't think those antibiotics have kicked in yet."

NINE

With Merle's red hands still clawing at him, Charlie crawled through the window

and jumped to the ground. Merle leaned out the window moaning and reaching.

Charlie stumbled toward us.

"Come on, maybe we can make it to my van."

"What about Daddy?"

He looked toward the window at my crazed father, still flailing at the window.

"I'm sorry, Cheyenne..."

"We can't just leave him here," I sobbed.

Charlie started to walk toward the parking lot.

"Well I sure as hell ain't taking him with us."

I ran toward the drive-through window.

"Daddy!" I cried, but he continued to moan and growl, his red, dilated eyes didn't even see me.

I felt Nicholas' arms reach around my shoulders, gently pulling me away.

"Come on, let's go."

For the first time I realized how strong Nicholas' body felt. I turned toward him and cried in huge ugly convulsions.

Nicholas stroked my hair gently, then pulled me by the arm, a little more firmly.

"Come on, we gotta catch up with your uncle."

"Okay," I wiped my nose on my sleeve and followed Nicholas out to the dark

parking lot.

"Where did he go?"

Nicholas' question was answered by Uncle Charlie's blood-curdling yell.

We followed the sound of his screams to where his van was parked.

I stopped short and gasped. Undead customers streamed in and out

of the van, gnawing

on pieces of raw meat while others shoved kibbles into their mouths

or tried to open cans

of cat and dog food by smashing them into the van.

Charlie grabbed at a customer right after it smashed his window with a cat food

can. The customer dropped the can then fastened his red hands

around Charlie's throat,

ready to go in for the bite.

Charlie pushed his hands against the Customer's head, trying to keep the teeth at bay.

"Cheyenne....shoot!"

"Well don't just stand there," I said to Nicholas. "You've got the gun, shoot him."

"Yeah, but aren't we supposed to conserve ammo?"

"SHOOT!" Charlie gasped.

Nicholas patted his pants, found the gun, then passed it to me.

"What are you doing?"

"You're a way better shot than me."

Charlie, about to faint, lost his grip on the customer's head.

I squeezed the trigger and the customer's head flew back in a spurt of blood. Its
body thudded to the ground.

Charlie held his throat, coughing.

A surge of adrenaline rushed through me. Part of me felt sick but another part of me felt like whatever else I did in my life would never equal what I

had just achieved in

that moment.

I was ready for more.

"Come on, let's get in the van!" I called and rushed to the

wood-paneled door.

"Wait! There might be--" I could hear Nicholas call after me,

but I ignored him.

I stepped inside the van and sure enough there was another

one of the creeps

behind the door. I clocked it with the gun and it started to stumble.

Uncle Charlie burst in.

"Watch out!" I cried, but it was too late.

The thing sunk its teeth into Uncle Charlie's neck. My

bravery and marksmanship

of two minutes ago was officially down the toilet.

Not satisfied, the zombie lunged at Charlie again. I hit it with

the gun.

Charlie grunted, holding his bleeding neck.

I clumsily turned the gun around and shot one round. It ricocheted off the wall, barely missing Nicholas as he entered the van. While Nicholas ducked I got off one more round, this time getting the customer in the ear. The freak stumbled, clutching its bleeding orifice. Nicholas shoved it out of the van and shut the door, locking it. I rushed to Uncle Charlie who was crouched in a fetal position, hands to his neck.

"Uncle Charlie, are you okay?"

"Yeah, can you drive this thing?"

Charlie heaved himself up to the dinette set and sat down. He reached into his jacket pocket, still keeping his other hand on his bleeding neck, pulled the van keys out of his pocket and tossed them at Nicholas.

The sound of hands pounding on the window thundered inside the tiny camper as it rocked beneath us.

"Can you drive this thing?" I asked.

Nicholas grabbed the keys from where they had fallen on the floor and scrambled

up to the cab.

"I can now."

I climbed up into the passenger seat. I happened to glance at the dashboard clock.

It said 11:35.

"Shit."

"What's the matter?" Nicholas asked as he fumbled with the keys.

"I forgot to call my mom...she's probably freaking out."

"We'll call her when we get some place safe--"

Beside me, the window filled with faces of infected customers.

Nicholas turned the key, pressed the gas and the van lurched forward.

Customers bounced off the windows while others continued to run alongside.

I looked out the window.

"Stop the car!" I yelled.

"What?"

"My mom, I see my mom's car!"

As customers ran at the van, Nicholas braked hard and they fell against the

windshield.

"Are you sure? This is a really bad time to stop."

"I'm sure. She just pulled in."

"Ok, call through the window and tell her it's not safe, tell her to go home."

I opened the door. I had to be able to get to her fast in case something happened.

"Mom!" I called.

"Shit, Cheyenne, I said the window..."

Mom saw me. She rolled down her window.

"Baby, are you OK? What's happening?"

I opened the door wider.

"Come on, get in!"

"No, what are you doing? Close the door!" Nicholas screamed.

Mom stuck her head out the window.

"What's happening? Who are all these...people?"

A customer stumbled toward Mom. Another approached my open door.

"Just get in the van, mom, and hurry up!"

The customer got to Darla's window, leaned over, and prepared to bite her.

I stepped out of the car. I had lost one parent that night. I wasn't about to lose another one.

"Mom...no!!!" I screamed as I ran out of the van towards my mother, desperate to save her from the claws of yet another marauding ghoul.

But Mom did something just then I didn't expect. She high kicked the bastard's face, spun and kicked it in the gut, then judo-flipped him.

Nicholas pulled me back in and shut the door. He auto-locked the door as another customer banged its head against the window. He stepped on the pedal and started to roar away.

"No, don't leave!"

I banged my fists against the window and watched as Mom kicked and karate chopped at the meat-corpse trying to eat her.

"Mom!" I yelled at the top of my lungs, even though I knew she couldn't hear me through the glass.

"Look she's gonna be Ok," Nicholas tried to sound reassuring. "We'll go back for her, I promise. We just need to get some help first..."

I felt the cold hard nose of the gun poking me in the waistband where I had stuck it after shooting the zombie that bit Uncle Charlie. I took it out and pointed it at Nicholas.

"Turn the van around," I said slowly, quietly.

"What are you doing?"

"What does it look like I'm doing? Turn the van around or I'm going to shoot you through the head."

"Cheyenne, take it easy!"

I fired a shot through the window, shattering it.

"Okay!!!"

Nicholas twirled the steering wheel in a desperate U-turn.

"Do you even know how many bullets are in that gun?"

"No, I just know I'm saving the last one for you."

He screeched to a stop.

"Okay, you can't just run out there, you've got to have a plan."

I reached across his lap, unlocked the doors and ran outside.

"Cheyenne!"

I ran through the parking lot still holding the gun. I could hear the pounding flap of Nicholas' sneakers behind me. Suddenly, the sneaker flapping stopped and I turned around. Dozens of infected customers circled around him.

"Shoot, Cheyenne!"

I looked at the gun in my hand.

"What if it's my last bullet?"

"Then we're dead anyway..."

I stared at the black steel in my hand as the customers shuffled closer, reaching toward me with outstretched hands. Nicholas reached into his waistband and pulled out his band baton. With a war cry, he ran toward the customer throng, banging the baton down hard on top of three zombie heads. The customers turned slowly and began to lunge toward him. Nicholas took the rubber top off his baton and threw it over his shoulder.

"Okay you shitheads, I'm gonna get all band-geek on your ass now."

Nicholas poked a customer in the forehead, leaving a bloody gash. He got another hard in the eye. SQUISH. The customer moaned and wandered off, his eye sliced. Nicholas poked another in the stomach and watched it double over.

Through the gap he created in the crowd, he reached toward me and pulled me towards him.

"Okay, I saved your life. Now no more pulling your gun on me, okay?" he smiled.

I leaned towards him. It was a weird place to flirt, but I was strangely digging it.

Until another body popped up between us: Dirk his eyes dead, face bloody. I clubbed him with the butt of my gun as hard as I could. Nicholas took a turn with his baton, but still the lunkhead wouldn't fall down. Finally, Nicholas shoved his baton through Dirk's stomach.

That did it.

Nicholas tried to pull the baton out of Dirk's stomach, but it was stuck.

"Oh no, what are we gonna do?"

We backed away from Dirk's body as customers continued to advance, trampling his corpse.

"I think you're gonna have to use that last bullet, Cheyenne."

I started to push at the zombies with my bare hands.

"Maybe I should just use it on myself..."

Nicholas grabbed me by the shoulders.

"No, don't ever say that. I won't let you do it, Cheyenne..."

"But before I do," I continued. "I didn't mean what I said back there, about saving the last bullet for you...and for the record, I would definitely go to the prom with you."

Nicholas pulled me towards him and kissed me. Softly, at first, and then harder, more insistent, even with a little bit of tongue; and at that moment I had the terrifying thought that this might be my first and last kiss. I felt dead hands clawing at my back, my hair. I let them. I didn't want the kiss to end.

Suddenly, bright lights shone in my eyes and a loud motor buzzed in my ears. The hands lifted themselves from my back and hair. I tore my lips away from Nicholas' and looked to see my mom's car driving straight through the crowd, sending bodies flying. She stopped right in front of us, rolled down the window, her hair a mess and headband askew, but otherwise perfectly fine.

"Get in the car!"

TEN

We dove into Mom's backseat, which was strewn with Fat Burner Energy Pill bottles and diet soda cans. I made sure to close and lock the door as the freaks slammed themselves into it. That didn't bother Mom; she just slammed the car into high gear.

"Mom, Dad got a hold of some bad meat--"

"That's one of his favorite hobbies," Mom said, not missing a beat as bodies flew off the windshield like gigantic bugs.

"No, I mean, he's infected, mom, and so is Uncle Charlie and everyone back there, they're all--"

Even though she was going about 85 miles an hour, she turned around and gave Nicholas the stink-eye.

"Well, if they're all infected why don't we shove him out of the car?"

"Mom!"

"Well, look at him! He's all orange and it's not like he tried to save my life."

"Sorry Mrs. M., I was just trying to save your daughter at all costs."

"That's Ms. M. and hey, it's nothing personal, just, I'm taking my daughter to Mexico and your parents might want you to stay and finish high school, that's all."

"Mom, are you crazy?" I cried. "Did you listen to a word I was saying?"

"Yes, I have been listening, Cheyenne, and I know how this all started."

"You do?"

"Yes, and it's all my fault."

We were out on the interstate now. Nothing but a long stretch of highway. Here and there I could see freaks stumbling along the roadside, but mom was driving so fast that soon it was just us, the asphalt and the moon.

Mom slowed a bit and settled into her seat as she began her tale:

"It was about 20 years ago at Monster Burger. Only it was called Quick Burger back then. Your dad was just the manager then. And Charlie was the fry cook. We all worked there. There was this guy, J.D. Christie, big high-school hot shot...He used to come in and mess with us; they all did. There was Richie...he loved to shoot spit-wads on the ceiling… then there was Barbara...she was blonde and had boobs the size of newborns. Oh, she was the worst of all...but J.D. was the one who paid for it.

One night they were in there and just made a big mess. Not only the spit-wads but shakes dumped on the floor, food and paper everywhere. And the worst thing was they would get the other kids to join in. Nice kids who just didn't want to look uncool in front of good ol' J.D. and his crew. So after they had all left and the place was empty, I noticed a set of keys on the counter. I knew they were his so I scooped them up and put them in my bra. He didn't miss them right away because Richie was driving. But the three of them must have gotten into some kind of tiff because Richie came back, dropped J.D. off in the parking lot and burned rubber out of there."

My mom stopped talking and let the hum of the engine and the tires smoothly colliding with the road fill the silence.

"So what happened then?"

"Well, the lights were out and the chairs were on the tables. J.D. pounds on the locked door, a little drunk, he teeters slightly and yells for us to let him in."

"Well, did you?"

"Yes, and I'll regret it for the rest of my life...I can't remember whose idea it was. Merle said as long as he was going to be alone with us we should mess with him a little bit. So Merle let him in and told him his keys were in the back. Charlie said we should put his shorts in the freezer. But in the end I think it was my idea. He had called me fat cow so many times I guess I just wanted to make him pay..."

Mom's voice broke. She sniffed. My God, was she actually going to cry? Never in my life had I seen her do that. Not when Grandma died, or her favorite cat or even when the divorce papers came in the mail.

"Wait a minute; he called *you* a fat cow?" Nicholas piped up.

"I didn't always look this good," Mom said wiping away a tear. "We used the element of surprise to our advantage. As J.D. came through to the back, Charlie threw an apron over his head and pulled the apron strings tight behind his neck. He never saw it coming...Merle punched J.D. in the stomach. As he doubled over, Merle shoved him into a chair and I went to work with the duct tape..."

"So what did you do to him?"

"At first nothing much. Oh, we called him a bunch of names. Tried to throw back in his face every insult he'd hurled at us. Trouble was, there wasn't much we could say bad about J.D. Christie. He was gorgeous, had perfect skin, an athlete's body. But he wasn't strong enough to get out of that duct tape, I was good...Well, finally, one of us, I don't remember who, got the idea to get a burger out of the garbage and shove it in his mouth and I said, 'Who's the fat cow now?' and then Merle grabbed one and did the same thing and so did Charlie...We had so much pent-up hatred inside us. It was like we had to get back at every mean thing that J.D. and his friends had done to us since the third grade."

"Well, gee Mrs. M, you didn't like kill him, did you?"

"No, not quite. I could still his chest rising and falling when we put him in the freezer."

"You put him in the freezer???" I cried. My thoughts went to Dirk. If he hadn't been a flesh-crazed zombie, there was no way I would have smashed his head in.

"Well, we had to; we weren't done cleaning up and what if he got out of that duct tape?"

The car went silent as we all contemplated what a screwed-up thing my parents had done.

"Oh, don't look at me like that. We'd locked ourselves in the freezer plenty of times...how do you think you were conceived, Cheyenne?"

I shoved that revolting image out of my head.

"After, you got him out of the freezer, mom, what happened, was he still alive?"

"Well, that was the funny thing. I guess with all that alcohol in his system and the cold and the food shoved down his throat, he wasn't...." it took her a few seconds to get the words out, "he wasn't breathing."

I couldn't even curse or yell at her. The look on her face told me of the years of pain she had endured.

We were just stupid kids. We didn't know CPR. Oh, yeah, we cleared the meat out of his mouth but that didn't do any good, so we loaded him in your dad's truck and dropped him off the ER.

"Wait a minute; you didn't go in with him? Or at least tell them what had happened?" it was Nicholas' turn to be indignant.

"And be charged with murder? I don't think so!" Mom spat. "And besides, we parked behind some bushes and some little orderly came out in just a few minutes."

Her voice broke and she let out a few heavy sobs. "They couldn't revive him. The doctors ruled it death by alcohol intoxication...he was really loaded that night."

"God, how awful, mom..."

"Don't you judge me!" she snapped, looking into the backseat. "I went to his gravesite every year on the anniversary of his death. We all did. Until Charlie got busy being a vet and Merle, well...anyway, I was all by myself there yesterday and I noticed something strange...there was a deep hole at the foot of J.D.'s grave."

ELEVEN

I leaned back in my seat, unable to believe much less comprehend what my mother was telling me.

Had she and my father really committed murder?

Part of me knew how they felt, knew that powerless rage when someone taunts you and humiliates you, but how could they just let him choke like that?

And now, could the guy be walking around among us—responsible for this zombie plague?

"Mom, why didn't you tell anyone?" I finally demanded.

"I tried to tell your father, but he wouldn't even answer his phone, and then I thought maybe J.D.'s parents had exhumed his body—"

"Not about the body, but why didn't you ever tell anyone what you had done?"

"And go to prison? Fat chance. And now with everything that's happened, I decided it would be a wonderful time to go to Mexico. Our flight leaves in an hour."

"Mom!" I cried. "We can't go to Mexico!"

She glanced toward Nicholas in the backseat.

"Fine, I'll try to put your little friend here on stand-by..."

"Mom!!!" I screamed again. But this time it wasn't because of her continued stupidity. It was because a man with a bloated body and peeling skin appeared in front of the car.

Mom screamed and hit the brakes, but the car slammed into the body anyway. Decaying skin filled the windshield.

She gassed it, but the man—if you could call it that—clung to the windshield, like a dead fly.

"GET HIM OFF! GET HIM OFF!" Mom screamed hysterically.

"Mom, just calm down. He's dead. He can't hurt you. Stop the car."

She eased off the accelerator and slowed to a stop. She put her head on the steering wheel and for the first time ever, I saw her body completely wracked with sobs.

Nicholas leaned forward and patted her shoulder.

"Everything's gonna be okay Mrs. M. Maybe if you just jam it into reverse and gas it, he'll fall off."

Mom, lifted her head, and seeing the dead eyes staring into the windshield, gave a deep shudder.

She pointed slowly, even while she looked away from the hideous face.

"You don't understand, th-that's him, that's…J.D."

Nicholas and I gaped for a moment at the face in the glass. Even after 20 years in the grave, his open mouth and wide bulging eyes still had the expression of someone who's got 24 pickles in his throat that just won't go down.

Mom slowly moved the gear shift lever into reverse, we all held our breath as she put her foot above the gas pedal.

Just then, J.D. opened his eyes and let out an inhuman yell. He punched the windshield and thousands of tiny shards of glass rained down into the front seat.

Mom screamed and slammed it into reverse. The car skidded wildly and I could hear the tires squealing as the car lost touch with gravity. In one unreal moment we were all upside down, J.D. still clinging to the windshield, only beneath us instead of on top of us. Then blackness engulfed us.

TWELVE

I opened my eyes to the sound of birds chirping.

It seemed like so long since I had heard that beautiful sound.

It seemed so long since I had seen sunlight.

There was a patch of it beside me on something that looked like grey grass.

It took me a full minute to realize it wasn't grass but the low pile carpet mat in the front seat of my mom's car.

Painfully, I raised my head and saw the empty passenger seat. Then I looked to the side and saw that the driver's seat was also vacant.

From somewhere, I heard a faint sound. Tap. Tap…..Tap.

Whatever it was, it was making my headache even worse.

I rubbed my temples and felt something liquid. I brought my fingers to my eyes. Blood. Fresh, red. I stared at it for a moment, wondering if it was my own.

Suddenly, the tapping became a loud CRUNCH.

I climbed up into the passenger seat and peered into the back. J.D. was gnawing on what appeared to be a leg bone. Beside him, Nicholas, or what was left of him, lay spread out on the backseat.

J.D. looked up at me. Or what used to be John David Christie, for in his eyes I saw only a bloodshot, dead stare.

I screamed, fumbled with the door, and jumped out of the car.

I took off running into the scrub. Behind me, I could hear his groan and lumbering footsteps.

I was making good time, even at my slow running pace, until I stumbled on a rock. I went down, pain shooting through the bone and muscle of my ankle.

When I finally got back up, he was closer, and his zombie stumble was becoming a full-bore run.

I limped away as fast as I could, grabbing at trees for support. But as I grabbed at one trunk, two arms grabbed for me. I started to swat them away, then realized it was my mother.

I collapsed into her arms, sobbing. She put her hand over my mouth, not comfortingly.

"Ssssh! He'll hear you!"

I tried as best I could to suck in my sobs. Sure enough, J.D., breathing

heavy and grunting, stumble-walked right on by us. Mom still waited a good minute or two before she finally took her hand off my mouth.

"He was eating Nicholas, mom, it was so awful…"

"We have to go after him."

"No, I want to go home. I want this

all to be over."

Mom took Dad's gun out of her waistband.

"It won't be over until we kill

him..."

I stared at the black revolver in her hand.

"You took Daddy's gun?"

"I'm trying to protect you, dear."

"You left me alone with that...thing and *you* took the gun?"

"I thought you were dead from the accident, there was no

time—"

"You're only out for yourself," I accused her.

"That's not true," she replied. "I'm going to kill him and save

the whole town, maybe the whole world—"

"You just know you have to because no matter where you

are he'll hunt you

down and kill you."

"No, honey, don't be like that."

I held out my palm.

"Give me the gun, mom."

"Honey, I really don't think—"

"Mom, I've shot four people today and I've only missed twice and one of

those times was on purpose."

She slowly handed the gun over to me.

"There might only be one bullet left. We want to do this right," I said, and started to head out into the clearing.

I looked behind me, expecting to see Mom, but she was still by the tree, laboring to get up, one of her legs bloody below the knee.

Suddenly, I felt weak. She may have been a bitch, but she was my mom and I was goddamned if I wanted to see her die.

"Mom," I ran over to her. "Oh my god, did he do that to you?"

"What, this?" she said, smiling. "It's just an old Zumba injury, you know, Livin' la Vida Loca..."

I draped her arm across my shoulder.

"Here, lean on me, just walk on your good leg."

She took her arm down.

"No. You said there might be only one bullet left. Use it on me. I don't

want to turn into one of them. I can't."

I tried not to let my voice break.

"You won't. This started with you and him, right? When we finish him off, this whole nightmare will be over, you'll see. Come on."

I looped my arm around my mother's waist and together we started off on the path.

I pulled her along for a quite a ways. There was no sign of Burgerbreath or any other zombies for that matter. It was just me and her. Step, drag. Step, drag.

Finally, she pulled away from me and went towards a tree. She fell onto it, vomiting.

She wiped her mouth, still heaving.

"I can't go on. Go do it yourself."

"But what if you need to be there to, you know, break the curse?" I asked.

She laughed.

"What curse? Maybe he was never really dead. Maybe none of us are

ever really gonna die. Just go finish him off."

I looked at her for a long moment. I didn't want to leave her there, but I knew she was stubborn. Like me.

"Okay, I'll come back for you, I promise," I finally said.

"Okay honey, I love you. Just the way you are," she said. I could see a tear starting in the corner of her eye.

"I love you, too, mom."

I turned my face away. I didn't want to let her see the tears forming in my eyes, because I knew if I looked at her one more time, they would never stop.

I took off running down the path then froze.

Ahead of me was the cemetery.

Dozens of undead pedestrians stumbled around the tombstones.

"Oh God, no--..." I said to myself.

I looked back toward where I had left my mother. The trail was empty.

I turned back towards the cemetery and stepped tentatively forward. As I approached the graveyard the moans became louder and the faces of the walking corpses became clearer: their once-red faces had faded to a dry mud red hue. I kept my eyes down, walking as if I was on a mine field.

They didn't seem to notice me at first, but then they tripped over in my direction, their unfocused eyes showing a reflexive arousal.

I continued to shuffle, halfway hoping if I walked like one of them, they would leave me alone. All the while, my eyes darted about, looking furtively for the bloated face of J.D.

Suddenly, I could feel something on my ankle. The pain of my sprain was immediately erased by the terror of feeling the long, gritty finger on my skin. I looked down and saw fingers coming up from the earth.

I shrieked and several pairs of eyes immediately shifted in my direction. I managed to yank my foot free, then I walked faster, still watching my step. The ghouls stumbled towards me with more urgency now.

I ducked to the right. It worked for a few seconds as they continued on to the left, but soon their eyes lit on me and they were coming my way again. I could see a new group of them coming out of a grove of trees. There must have been forty or fifty of them.

I broke into a run.

Beyond me, I could see a gate. A green field. No zombies.

I ran faster. Eyes on the wrought-iron door to my freedom. Then the ground beneath me suddenly began to sink. I fell, dropping my gun on the grass. I scrambled to get it back but everything was sinking: the earth, the grass. The last thing I saw was the tombstone: J.D. Christie.

THIRTEEN

Screaming, I landed in the hole. In the dim light, I could see J.D. lying on his back, eyes closed. I stopped screaming and stared at him.

Maybe he was already dead.

Suddenly, his eyes snapped open.

I screamed, loud primal shrieks, as I reached up clawing dirt, scrambling to get out.

J.D. sat up. Then, propping himself up one leg at a time, he stood up. I stopped clawing at the sides of the hole as he came towards me. There were just inches between us. Before I knew what

I was doing, I copied one of mom's karate kicks and got him in the mouth. White shards of teeth flew out of his mouth.

Momentarily stunned, he continued to close in on me. I clawed some more at the wall of the hole, like a cat, desperate to get out of a giant litter box. My fingers hit something hard. A rock. I managed to dig at it while kicking J.D. at the same time. He came back for more, just as I got the small boulder loose. I pounded him in the head with it.

He gave an angry, muffled moan and grabbed my arm. He was about to bite, but I yanked my arm away. I stuck my foot in the hole where the rock had been, and lifted myself up. But all I could do was claw at the upper reaches of the hole. There was nowhere to go.

Earth from above started to dump in on me as J.D. grabbed at my leg. All I could do was kick to keep him from getting a mouth-hold.

As the avalanche continued, I saw the gun go falling past me. It landed on the bottom of the hole. I looked down at it, debating whether I should go down and retrieve it or keep trying to climb up. I finally made up my mind, gave J.D. a good boot to the head, and jumped down to pick up the gun.

I aimed it straight at his head.

"I'm sorry for what my mom and dad did to you, but now it's time for you to die."

I pulled the trigger and was greeted by an empty click.

I pulled it some more, frantically, then gave up and just hit him in the head with the gun. It didn't seem to faze him, just made him zombie-angry. He grabbed my neck
and started to strangle me.

I hope I never feel that sensation again. I couldn't gasp. I couldn't choke. Just silence as I felt the air and the life being sucked out of me.

I felt myself being lifted up off the ground. I saw his wide pasty dead mouth and its bloody teeth, getting ready to bite.

I could feel myself starting to black out even as I dangled, but then something reached my ears. A jingling sound. Dad's keys.

With my last bit of strength, I dug into my pocket, took them out and jabbed them as hard as I could into J.D.'s forehead.

As he released me and I fell, air went violently back into my lungs. When I finished coughing I looked up to see J.D. falling back, keys stuck in his frontal lobe.

But I wasn't satisfied. Still coughing and rubbing my neck, I stood up over his body and stomped down on the keys so they buried deep into his skin with a squelch.

His eyes rolled back in his head. I looked at him in horrified fascination as the skin started to fall from his face. Muscle was revealed, but it too became dry as a bone and fluttered off like sand in a dust storm. Soon, he was nothing but a skeleton.

I reached down and grabbed the keys from the crack in his skull. Those keys were the only thing left I had of my dad. As the skull split in half, dry sand poured out.

I stuck my foot back in the hole and reached up, using the keys as a dysfunctional piton. I think in the end it was my arms. My fat jiggly arms. I willed them to pull the rest of my fat jiggly body out of that hole and then I sat down beside it and cried. I wailed I sobbed. I didn't even realize that the zombies that had been chasing me were all running away, back toward the grove of dark, dense trees.

It could have been the fat burner energy immunity still burning through my system. Maybe it was fear—if zombies can feel such a thing. Call it self-preservation. They knew I had just kicked the toughest zombie butt in the whole cemetery and they were running for their unlives. But I wanted to believe I had broken the curse. I had to believe it. That when I got back to that tree where I left my mom, she would be back to her skinny, tan with a hint of blush-faced self. And I could go back to the car and find Nicholas, practicing his baton or touching up his tan. The whole night would be like a bad dream that would just go away.

I got to my feet, sore and bruised; I limped across that dead, green deathfield as the morning mist rose off the graves. I hurried as fast as I could, out of the funeral gates to the wild trees. They all looked the same now. Why didn't I leave a trail of crumbs? I went from tree to tree, not even bothering to move slowly in case one of J.D.'s Undead Army was still lurking about. There was no one. Nothing. Even the birds had stopped singing.

Then I saw it. Her headband. The red-white-and-blue one she always wore. She wanted to look like Bruce Springsteen, I guess. Or that hot babe Bruce Springsteen dumped his wife for back in the 80's, was what she always told me. That's my mom. Totally retro.

I bent over, picked up the headband, held it to my face. If she had been attacked, they would have left more than this. Probably a fibula or a scapula, at least. No, this seemed like it was done with a purpose. It was a sign to me. It said Daughter, don't give up hope, keep looking.

I ignored the pain in my ankle and ran down the slope to the car. I didn't dread seeing the scene of carnage that I had left what seemed like years ago there, because sure enough, he was gone. Of course, there were still blood-stains all over the backseat, but no entrails, no exposed bones. It was like Nicholas had tucked himself back inside himself and just walked away.

And what about Daddy? Had his skin changed from red to orange then back to olive brown like mine? Maybe he was back in the joint already, flipping burgers. Regular ones this time, not monster meat.

I gave a little whoop and fist pump. For the first time in 24 hours...no, the first time in I don't know how long, I had a new feeling.

Hope.